Tuttle the Octopus
Coral Reef Birthday Adventure

Written and Illustrated by

Caren Eckrich

ACKNOWLEDGMENTS

To my husband for always believing in me. To my kids for keeping me young. To my mom for being so positive. To the people I've taught – you remind me of how special it is to experience something for the first time. To my fellow reef lovers for doing their best to protect coral reefs against many threats. To coral reefs around the earth and the precious critters that live within – thank you for the privilege of getting to know you.

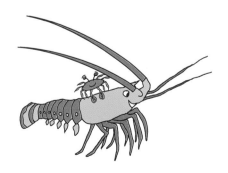

Early one morning on a colorful coral reef

Tuttle was the first one awake, to her great relief.

You see, it was her children's birthday, all eight,

And birthdays were special, not just presents and cake,

But a day full of fun and adventure and birthday wishes.

No school, no homework, no doing the dishes!

As the young octopuses awoke, excitement filled their den.

They realized their birthday was finally upon them!

They each would choose their favorite thing to do

And off they would go all yelling, "Yahoo!"

But first Tuttle gave them sponge cake to eat

And for small octopuses, this was a treat!

Who would go first? They quickly agreed

Alphabetical order was the best way to proceed:

Annabelle, Bonnie, Isabelle and Frans,

Jacob, Ocean, Storm and Yolande.

Annabelle was first and she quickly decided.

"To the Christmas Tree Forest!" and off they glided.

It wasn't long before they were surrounded

By Christmas tree worms all pointed and rounded.

The beautiful worms were dainty and swirled

Each with a small tube, slender and curled.

As each small octopus waved each octopus arm,

The worms would react with much alarm.

Into their tubes they would rapidly whirl.

Then, a bit later, they would slowly unfurl.

As the octopuses wiggled and jiggled,

Worms would disappear and octopuses giggled.

This was just the beginning of their special day

It was now time for Bonnie to lead the way.

Since she could remember, her dearest wish

was to have tea with Maxima the Queen Parrotfish.

Tuttle had once helped the Queen and won her favor

By inking a shark that preferred parrotfish flavor.

Tuttle had been given a royal invitation from the queen

and the palace was the most beautiful place they had ever seen.

They were so excited, their arms were all a'flutter.

As they met the queen, it was hard not to stutter.

The tea was divine and the crab cakes were yummy

The perfect combination for a hungry tummy.

The octopuses finished and wiped their faces clean

Then they bowed very low and thanked the pretty queen.

Next was Isabelle's turn to choose what to do.

It was no surprise – her wish everyone knew.

They would visit the best storyteller of all.

Makayla the Moray would excite and enthrall.

She lived deep in a crevice in the coral reef.

She was big and green and had long sharp teeth.

Most octopuses would stay far away

From an enormous, green, toothy moray!

But Makayla loved Tuttle and her kids – all eight

For they had good manners and were never late.

Makayla welcomed them and gave them all a hug.

They sat down on sea bean bags spread out on the rug.

She told them a story about two mermaids she had met,

Two sisters, Zani and Birgit, who were very upset.

They had long flowing hair and glittery scales

On their long and beautiful mermaid tails.

The mermaids had gotten lost in a forest of kelp

and wanted to go home, but needed help.

Makayla was old and wise and very witty

She knew the location of the secret mermaid city.

Makayla told the octopuses of her travels with the sisters,

About getting stuck in quicksand and about getting blisters.

The mermaid parents were so happy to see their lost girls

That they gave Makayla a pretty necklace made of pearls.

The octopuses oohed and aahed and had questions galore

Then they hugged goodbye and left through her large, round door.

For his wish, Frans knew exactly where to go

To a cool dance club that was way down below.

They swam through tunnels with glow worms a-glowing

and reached the dance floor where the music was flowing!

Snapping Shrimp set the beat with some groovy snapping.

Mantas started flapping and everyone began clapping.

Sander the Spotted Drum was drumming,

Trumpetfish was playing and Guitarfish was strumming,

and Wilfred the Whale was singing and humming.

The octopuses went wild dancing octopus style.

They boogied and bumped and spun and jumped for quite a while!

When the band took a break the excitement subsided.

It was time to move on the octopuses decided.

Next it was Jacob's turn to lead the way.

He led them to a place where they used to play.

A place they now sadly called garbage bay.

For humans had also discovered this place.

Some people were clean and wouldn't leave a trace

But others left tons of trash - what a disgrace!

Jacob was very keen on reef clean-ups

So they collected bottles, bags & cups.

They cleaned until the bay was beautiful once more...

at least until humans came again to that shore.

Tuttle's family now gave Ocean her chance

To visit the dancing seahorses and watch them prance.

The seahorses were red, yellow, green and black

they were always hungry and begged for a snack.

The octopuses collected tasty seagrass nearby

& fed it to the seahorses in exchange for a ride.

Each of them chose a friendly seahorse to ride

and off they went, matching stride for stride.

They explored crab canyon and anemone alley

and saw an old ghost wreck as their finale.

They slid off and thanked and pet each seahorse.

They promised to visit again soon, of course!

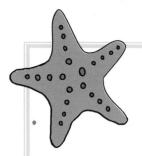

Then Storm yelled, "let's not dilly dally

Off we go to play in sponge valley!"

Until now, they had been too young and too small

Sponge jumping was risky – you could fall!

Storm went first. Tuttle stuck him deep in a tube...

The sponge pumped and pumped until out he flew!

He deftly bounced from sponge to sponge

It was scary and exciting and so much fun!

Soon all of the octopuses were happily sponging

All over the place octopuses were wildly plunging!

Tube sponges, barrel sponges, ball sponges and more

They jumped from them all – there were sponges galore!

It wasn't long until the octopuses were tired

But then Storm had an idea and they all were inspired.

With sponges in the background, they played hide-and-seek

and since octopuses change color, it's easy to sneak!

Suddenly Tuttle stopped and saw far in the deep

a large sea turtle beginning to weep.

His name was Jorg and he was caught in a net

He couldn't breathe and was very upset!

A fisherman had left his net unattended.

For turtles and birds this is NOT recommended!

So Tuttle and her kids began biting and ripping

Through the net until Jorg's flippers were flipping.

Up, up they helped him swim to the surface

To gulp fresh air and breathe with purpose.

They had saved his life and he was so happy

He thanked them and swam away perky and flappy.

The octopuses waved good-bye and they all agreed

That some humans must not care about animals' needs.

Their special day was quickly drawing to a close

Some of the octopuses were starting to doze.

But the smallest birthday octopus, Yolande,

Would choose an activity of which she was fond.

Oddly, since she was born, she had always dreamed

of being completely and thoroughly cleaned!

It wasn't a far swim to a place Tuttle knew

The Caribbean Cleaning Station - this would do!

Small fish and shrimp picked & scrubbed and preened

Until each little octopus was utterly clean!

It was ticklish & silly and so much fun

They were all a bit sad when the cleaning was done.

It was getting dark and it was time to end their play.

It had been an awesome and fabulous birthday!

They were so tired that their faces were sagging.

They headed to their den with their tentacles dragging.

Tuttle fed her hungry kids Lobster a la Zeus

And finished it off with fresh seagrape juice.

They thanked her for the best birthday there could ever be

And agreed that Tuttle was the best mom in the sea!

They spoke of each adventure with delight

As Tuttle kissed each little octopus goodnight.

That evening she was reminded of her firm belief:

there was no better place to live than the coral reef.

ABOUT THE AUTHOR

Caren Eckrich grew up in Texas and moved to the Caribbean for her graduate studies in marine biology in Puerto Rico. She lived on an old sailboat and when she graduated, she sailed to the small island of Bonaire where she fell in love with the island, the coral reefs and a very handsome Dutch man. For fifteen years she ran a marine education center, Sea & Discover, that offered coral reef snorkeling and diving programs to children and adults. She also taught coral reef ecology and scientific diving to university study abroad students. Tuttle the Octopus Coral Reef Adventure is Caren's first children's book and was largely inspired by her and her family's experiences with and love of coral reefs.

Color this page and circle all of the things
that don't belong on the coral reef.

44361798R00019

Made in the USA
Charleston, SC
27 July 2015